Hi F
Thanks o

MW00944474

rt!

Merry Christmas

Love,
Janet M.

12/18/2021

Elizabeth
and the Piccadilly Council
When Buckingham Calls

Written by
anet McCarroll

Illustrator
Turine Tran

Elizabeth and the Piccadilly Council
When Buckingham Calls

©2021 Janet McCarroll

ISBN: 978-1-09839-743-2

Acknowledgments

To J.M. Gregory— all I can say is thanks for absolutely everything. It's been one heck of a ride, my dear.

To all of my cherished animals— thank you for being part of my inspiration and for being my family. Each of you has taught me how to consider the perspective of others more than anyone else possibly could have.

To Penn Mullin— this project really brings our first introduction long ago full circle. So eternally grateful to have you in my life, and to have you as a writing mentor, and as part of the Piccadilly team.

To Thomas Lee Coates— thank you for reminding me that all of life's answers can be found in a great story and for encouraging me to create stories of my own to share with others. I'll continue making the transcending journey to your beloved "Dreamland" for us both.

To Queen Elizabeth II— thank you for being such a captivating monarch. You have truly been a joy to write about. And thanks for being a great example to girls and world leaders everywhere.

And thank you to everyone else who has loved, encouraged, or inspired me. Most of you know who you are.

Table of Contents

CHAPTER ONE

All Things Must Change

On this jolly old day in England, a little girl about ten years old, and eloquently dressed in a light-blue horse-riding uniform, was driven along in a chauffeured shiny cobalt-blue car. Down the streets of London, the car traveled as she poked her head out of the back window to enjoy the cool autumn air. The only thing that was keeping the gentle wind from blowing her brown hair into her face was a blue barrette that she was wearing to match her riding outfit. She had borrowed the barrette from her younger sister, who had kindly lent it to her. Her sister knew that she liked all of her outfits to match.

As the car neared home, the girl got more excited. She couldn't wait to get back to the house and tell her family how well her riding lesson had gone. She had been at the nearby stables practically all day. Her father usually attended her lessons, as he took great delight in watching his daughter excel at the sport she ever so loved, but lately, he seemed distracted and agitated—worried in fact. Nevertheless, she was sure that the news of her riding progress would bring her father much-needed joy. Since everyone else in the family also seemed to be busy, she instead had taken the family Corgi—Winston. He now had his head out of the window too. He seemed just as excited about her good news as she did. Vernon, the family chauffeur, could see from his rear-view mirror that his passengers were getting anxious.

"All right, you two Royal Highnesses," he said jokingly, "I know you're eager to get home and tell everyone all about today; we'll be home any minute."

Vernon's words were ever so precise, for in what seemed to be exactly one minute, the car arrived right in front of 145 Piccadilly, the only home the young Princess and her royal pooch had ever known.

"What's this?" Vernon proclaimed as he arched his neck to see what was going on out of his window.

"Vernon, why is a photographer here?" asked the Princess, who had spotted the professional-looking man standing outside the gates to her family home, holding what looked like a very large and expensive piece of camera equipment.

"Your Grace," Vernon said in a very concerned tone that matched his facial expression, "roll up your window at once."

The Princess, who was usually an obedient girl, felt the rare urge to ignore Vernon's request. But it was even rarer for

Vernon to request anything of her, especially given her status. She knew that it must have been serious enough for him to require her compliance. The Princess took one last look at the man holding the camera who was about to turn around and notice her and then rolled up her window as quickly as possible. She thought that by doing so, Vernon's face would return to its commonly jovial and peaceful way of being, but the concerned look remained. It didn't help tensions in the car that Winston was now barking at the man with the camera whom they had just driven past. The noise made Vernon crinkle his right eyebrow, something he did only under stress, which was almost never. Trying to clamp Winston's snout with her right hand and holding him by the collar with her left, the Princess dug her heels into the floor of the car in order to stay seated as Vernon swerved the car into the driveway of the York family home. He made the turn quickly enough to avoid someone spotting them, just in case anyone else was lurking in the area. The Princess was so excited to be home, she threw the back car door open just as Vernon was about to open it for her, and she and Winston hopped out of the back seat. Forgetting all about the photographer she'd seen, the girl ran toward a little side door that was attached to the very large home. But just before she could open the door, Emmaline Crawford, the family's nanny, opened it up.

"Shhhh, Your Royal Highness," she said, "be very quiet as you enter the house; a lot is happening at the moment."

The Princess nodded her head at Emmaline's request and made her way up the stairs into the family's living quarters with Winston leading the way. She found her mother pacing outside of her father's office door that was slightly cracked open. Her mother, very fancily dressed, turned and looked at her.

"Mother, I must tell you about my day with the horses!" she exclaimed.

"Shhh, Elizabeth," her mother hushed in a tone like Emmaline's, with a look on her face identical to that of Vernon.

Elizabeth inhaled deeply. She could hear hostile rambling coming from inside of her father's office. Other than the words "absurd," "selfish," and "that woman," she couldn't make out anything else her father was saying. Elizabeth could feel something was not only wrong but also different.

"Mother, where is Margaret?" she asked.

"Shhh," her mother snapped.

"Well, what's going on?" Elizabeth continued to ask.

"Emmaline, please," her mother begged, "take the child to her room at once!"

"Yes ma'am, right away ma'am," Emmaline responded.

Emmaline rushed over behind Elizabeth and gently pushed her by the shoulders in the direction of her room. She guided Elizabeth by the shoulders through the kitchen, across the parlor, past the terrace doors, up three long flights of stairs, down two long hallways, and straight into her bedroom. "Now, you stay here," insisted Emmaline with a stern face, "and change out of your riding clothes."

"Okay," Elizabeth sighed. Emmaline's tense face soon turned into a gentle smile as she gave the girl a pinch on the cheek that got a giggle out of Elizabeth. The nanny turned and walked out of the room, making sure to close the door behind her. Elizabeth sat on a small cushion by the door and placed her chin in between her palms. Just when she thought she had a moment alone, the door slightly cracked open, and Emmaline's hand could be seen reaching in the doorway, guiding Winston into the room by the collar. The door shut behind him as he ran over to sit by Elizabeth's leg. Elizabeth reached down to pet him behind the ears.

"What's going on around here, Winston?" she asked. Winston looked up at her almost as if he was trying to answer the question. Thus far, it was Winston who had made more effort to clue her in than anyone else. "Well," she said as she stood up, "I'd better change into my day clothes."

Elizabeth made her way over to the closet. Just as she began perusing, a lightbulb went off in her head. She knew exactly who could help her. Elizabeth climbed upon a wooden shelf in the closet. Standing atop the shelf, she leaned over to an iron-grate furnace and spoke into it. "Come in, Margaret. Are you there? Margaret, are you there? I'm calling a meeting here in the flagship room, do you read?"

Elizabeth then climbed down from the shelf. She stood in silence, biting down on her lower lip, uncertain if her younger sister had received the urgent message. In an instant, Winston started barking at the sound of Elizabeth's bookcase as it began making a creaking noise. The bookcase was situated next to her closet. The right end of the shelving moved forward, revealing a tiny, awkwardly shaped door that was almost ancient in appearance. The small door shoved open and a little, bright-eyed girl with brown, shoulder-length hair popped her head out of the narrow passageway.

"Hi, Lilibet. When'd you get home?" Margaret asked in a high-pitched voice. Elizabeth kneeled down to help pull her sister through the small passageway. The crawl space leading to each other's rooms was becoming harder to get through as they got bigger, but it was still handy for emergencies. After assisting Margaret, Elizabeth ran across the room to lock her bedroom door. The small passageway was a secret; not even Emmaline knew about it. The family had lived in the house for years, and her parents knew every nook and cranny—but the passageway continued to remain a secret all this time. Elizabeth and her younger sister sat by the bedroom window.

"How'd your riding lesson go today?" Margaret innocently asked. "Did you get to ride Peppermill again?"

"Not now," Elizabeth hissed. She was usually pleased when someone took an interest in her riding, but now was no time to talk about horses.

"Margaret, listen, I need you to tell me about what's been going on," she pressed.

"Gosh, Lilibet, I don't know."

"But ever since I got home," Elizabeth continued, "everyone has been acting strangely."

"I don't know what to tell you, Lil," said Margaret, "I really don't know anything."

Elizabeth took a long doubtful look at her younger sister, who resembled her in every way, except that Margaret had a mischievous twinkle in her eye that Elizabeth did not have, and she also had a missing front tooth.

"Margaret, I don't believe you," Elizabeth fussed. "Come on, you mean you haven't listened in on Mother's gossip, you haven't gotten any tip-offs from the butler, or you haven't slipped into Father's office to eavesdrop even once today when no one was looking?"

"Nope," Margaret said casually as she stood up from where she was sitting.

"Well, did you at least hear something during your piano lesson?"

"Nothing," Margaret said. "My lesson was to be at noon today, but Mother had Emmaline tell the instructor not to come."

Elizabeth jumped to her feet in a gasp. "Why would they do a thing like that? After all, they let me go to my riding lesson today."

"I know," said Margaret. "At first, I figured it was because you're older, but then I realized that it was because you left earlier. It wasn't until around 10 o'clock this morning that Father said no one was to either leave the house or come to the house."

"Why would that be?" asked Elizabeth.

"How should I know?" replied Margaret. "I'm only six. Alls I know is that Father said Uncle Eddie has gone mad."

"They've been fighting a lot lately," Elizabeth said.

"I know," replied Margaret, "and it's getting worse."

"That's not like them," continued Elizabeth, "Father loves Uncle Edward. Something must really be wrong." The two girls shook their heads in agreement. Elizabeth pulled

Margaret close, both girls feeling uncertain of what was to come.

"If Father and Uncle Eddie don't make up soon, do you think Uncle Eddie will still come to your birthday party in April?" Margaret asked, looking up at a worried Elizabeth.

Elizabeth adoringly snickered in disbelief over what Margaret had just asked. She often times felt that her sister was much cleverer than she gave herself credit for.

"Girls," called Emmaline from the hallway. "I need you to get ready for tea."

Elizabeth looked down and realized that she hadn't changed out of her riding clothes, not to mention, their secret passageway ran the risk of being exposed! All the chaos made Winston bark again. "Go back to your room!" instructed Elizabeth. "I'll see you at dinner."

"I'm out of here," said Margaret as she rushed back to the tiny doorway.

That night Elizabeth was too antsy to sleep alone, so she decided to sleep in Margaret's bed.

"Lil, don't you find it odd that neither Mother nor Father joined us for tea this evening?" asked Margaret.

"Yes, I do," replied Elizabeth. Her voice sounded calmer than her nerves actually were. She was out of answers, and she didn't know what to make of her family's recent peculiar behavior. "Don't worry, Margaret, things will be back to normal soon," Elizabeth promised her sister. But the truth be told, Margaret wasn't the one who was worried, Elizabeth was.

Elizabeth finally fell asleep by convincing herself that things would be as usual in the morning. But things weren't as usual the next morning. In fact, the opposite happened. The uproar at 145 Piccadilly continued for days. Every time Elizabeth looked outside of her bedroom window, a new photographer was standing outside of their family home. Their mother, the Duchess of York, continued to pace outside of her father's office. Still, no one was allowed to go to or from the house. However, Elizabeth's grandmother, Mary, would arrive unannounced from time to time. The Duke, Duchess, and Queen Mary would rant and rave on and on about Uncle Eddie—how irresponsible he was being, how unroyal his behavior was becoming, and how a hit from Cupid's arrow was clouding his better judgment. The worse things got, the more her father yelled from his office, and the more he yelled, the worse his stutter got. All the while, Vernon's right eyebrow had become permanently crinkled.

CHAPTER TWO

No Going Back

Then, on a Wednesday morning, Elizabeth overheard her grandmother talking to her mother and father in the dining room. "Really, Albert, it's far beyond time that you tell the children. They need to know, especially Lilibet."

"Tell us what?" Elizabeth spoke from outside of the doorway. She shyly peeked out from around the door and sheepishly walked into the dining room, still wearing her nightgown. She was hoping to avoid a scolding for being up so early and for listening in on an adult conversation. Her mother, father, and grandmother—all sat around a bare dining room table. Sitting along with them was Emmaline, a man by the name of Sir Reginald Phifer, and Prime Minister Stanley Baldwin. She recognized Sir Reginald right away, as he had been serving as an advisor to her Uncle Eddie and even to her grandfather before that.

"I thought no one was allowed to the house," inquired Elizabeth. Curiosity had gotten the better of Elizabeth and that fueled her courage to speak up.

"Hello, Your Highness," said Mr. Baldwin. Both he and Sir Reginald Phifer stood up to acknowledge her presence.

"Your Highness," said Sir Reginald, as he tipped his hat. Sir Reginald had always addressed Elizabeth as Your Highness, but this time he said it with a level of conviction that Elizabeth was not accustomed to.

"Come here, Lilibet," insisted her grandmother. Elizabeth moved further into the room before continuing to speak. "Grandmother, why is everyone here?"

Queen Mary took her granddaughter's hand and looked at her as if to be taken aback by how young and blameless the girl was. It was like she was looking at Elizabeth for the first time.

"Albert, now is just as good of a time to tell her as any," Grandmother Mary urged.

Elizabeth looked over at her father, his eyes were red, dreary, and damp. It scared Elizabeth to think that her father had been sobbing. He paused for a moment to collect his thoughts and then spoke. "Y-y-you see, d-dear," he stammered, "w-w-we-we're moving."

Elizabeth's eyes widened at the news she had just received. "Moving, Father, moving? Moving where? Are we going to White Lodge or something?"

White Lodge had been her grandmother's countryside home for several years.

"No, child, you won't be moving to White Lodge," her grandmother intervened. "You'll be moving to the palace; your father is now needed there."

"Buckingham!" blurted out Elizabeth.

At this point, Elizabeth's family were the only ones looking directly at her. Everyone else in the room did their best to look away.

"But, Father, I love Piccadilly, and so do you. I don't want to leave, and Mother wouldn't want to either. Right, Mother?" she asked, looking over to her mother for reinforcement.

"Oh, Lilibet, this one is out of our hands," her mother replied.

"But," Elizabeth continued.

"Make no more fuss, child," said Grandmother Mary. "It's what has to happen."

"Well, this might be the silliest thing I've ever heard of," Elizabeth cried out. "Besides, there'd hardly be room for us there. What would Uncle Eddie want with Margaret and myself running about the palace all the time? Not to mention, Winston will destroy the new tulips he just had planted."

"Your Uncle Edward will no longer be living at the palace," said her mother.

"Believe me, my dear girl, we are just as dismayed as you are," Mr. Baldwin chimed in. He and Sir Reginald Phifer stood up once again and walked toward the door. Her father and mother stood up as well to escort the two gentlemen out of the room. Elizabeth hopped into her grandmother's lap as she watched them leave. She could still hear the grownups talking outside of the dining-room door.

"I'm truly sorry," said Sir Reginald Phifer to her father. "There's just nothing else we can do."

The Duke nodded his head in a hopeless manner as if everything was out of his control.

"Be sure to tune in on Friday," said Mr. Baldwin. "The whole world will be tuning in I can assure you."

The two men tilted their hats to the Duke and Duchess, and then left the 145 Piccadilly home through the side door of the house. Elizabeth climbed down from her grandmother's lap and sprinted to find Margaret. She didn't know every detail just yet, but she knew enough on the matter to clue her sister in.

The morning of Friday, December 11, 1936 came. Elizabeth and her family did what so many families around jolly old England did that very same morning. They listened to King Edward addressing his nation for what would be the last time. Elizabeth and Margaret scurried into the living room to join the gathering around the radio. Only her father wasn't there to share the moment, he had left home on business. But everyone else in the house, including her mother, grandmother, Vernon, and Emmaline, waited around the radio to hear Uncle Eddie's speech.

"Bark- bark!" Winston called out.

"Silence, Winston!" Grandmother Mary snapped.

"This is it, it's on," Elizabeth's mother said anxiously.

"This is Windsor Castle," said the radio presenter, "and now, here to make a speech, is His Royal Highness, King Edward."

"Oh, Uncle Eddie's about to speak," applauded Margaret.

Elizabeth covered Margaret's mouth to make sure that nothing Uncle Eddie said went unheard. Uncle Eddie went on and on about stepping down from his royal duties and allowing his younger brother, the Duke of York Prince Albert to become the king instead. Abdication, he insisted, would allow him to marry the woman whom he loved.

This is really happening to us, Elizabeth thought to herself.

Grandmother Mary shook her head in despair as she rocked herself back and forth. "I can never forgive him for this," she moaned. "What is that boy thinking? What would his father say? Thank goodness for Albert," she went on, "if it weren't for my darling Bertie, I'd have no sensible children."

"You mean Uncle Eddie's leaving everything behind just so he can get hitched?" Margaret questioned. "Boy, he really has gone mad."

Elizabeth covered Margaret's mouth again, but this time it was because she didn't want Margaret's words to upset their very distraught grandmother more.

That night Elizabeth couldn't sleep yet again, so she slept in Margaret's room once more for solace. At first, she thought Margaret was asleep, but Margaret was wide awake and had a lot to say about the day's events.

"Do you think Uncle Eddie will move to America with his new wife?" she asked.

"I don't know," said Elizabeth. "I suspect she'll be longing to move back home."

"Maybe he and Ms. Simpson will let me play the piano for them at their wedding," Margaret enthusiastically gushed.

"Yes, maybe," Elizabeth said. She knew this was highly unlikely, but she didn't have the heart to squash her little sister's ambitions.

The room was silent for a few moments, and then Margaret sat back up. "Oh Lilibet, my gosh! Do you know what I just realized?"

"What?" asked Elizabeth.

"We don't have a brother."

"I know that silly," scoffed Elizabeth.

"And you're the oldest," Margaret continued. Elizabeth could tell where Margaret was going with this and it was a thought she had long been trying to block out.

"Oh, sissy, think about it," Margaret harped on. "If Father is going to be king, this means one day you'll be the queen."

"Shhh!" Elizabeth hushed. "There's no use in thinking about something so far away now. We've only got a few nights left here at Piccadilly; let's just enjoy it."

"Okay," Margaret surrendered and lay back down in another attempt to sleep. But she just couldn't shake the excitement of it all. "You'll be a great queen you know, probably the best there ever was."

"You think so?" asked Elizabeth.

"Sure I do," replied Margaret. "Just watch, they'll call you Elizabeth the Great one day, you'll see." Margaret's love and certainty made Elizabeth feel a little more at ease about whatever the future might bring.

"Thanks, Margaret," Elizabeth said, kissing her sister on the forehead. And the two girls fell fast asleep.

Moving day came, and Elizabeth had finished packing her room up faster than everyone else. This was not because she was eager to move, but because she wanted enough time to make sure that her things were packed in a neat and orderly manner. This was to ensure that none of her belongings got lost in the moving process. She was especially watchful over the trunk containing her toy horse collection. Elizabeth sat in her bedroom window, dressed in a misty blue winter coat and a wide-brimmed hat turned up in front. She felt sort of dazed, but she was trying to endure the day for her family's sake. Elizabeth was just about to go over to her bookcase and access the secret passageway to her sisters' room one last time when Emmaline flung her bedroom door open in a panic. "Elizabeth, there you are, thank goodness. Have you seen that naughty little sister of yours?"

"No," answered Elizabeth. "I was actually just on my way to her room. She needed help packing a few of her last things."

"Well, I'm afraid she has chosen today of all days to play hide-and-go-seek. No one has seen her since breakfast." Emmaline slapped her palm to her forehead. Her face was tomato red from the unwanted last-minute task of having to find Margaret. "Of all the days, why would she choose today?" muttered Emmaline as she stormed off down the hall in search of the already infamous princess. *Well, if Margaret is missing, then I might as well take one last look around the house,* Elizabeth thought to herself. And so she did just that. She trekked around the entire house and was sure to take in every square inch and every spare detail. She noticed how there was not even one Christmas decoration anywhere to be found in the house. With all of the unplanned family events and the untimely rush of her father's succession, nobody had had enough time to put up so much so as a jingle bell.

She made her way to the outside grounds and loitered around every open space. Every cobblestone and flower bed held an abundance of memories for her. She came to an area where she and Margaret had built a small wooden fort to play in a few years back. Glass mosaic stepping stones that Emmaline had helped them make went around the whole fixture. Castle York, as the girls called it, sat surrounded by all sorts of plants and flowers that were fragrant in summer.

Elizabeth thought about how it had taken her sister and her days to decorate the inside of the castle. She looked over at the sprawling croquet pitch that her mother and father had put in for them just that spring past. As she stood in the family garden, her daydreams of past times were interrupted by the foggy faint sound of someone calling her name.

Just when she realized whose voice it was, Margaret ran up behind her and grabbed her by the hand. "Lilibet, come on," Margaret insisted as she tugged on her elder sister's hand while clutching her teddy bear in the other. "Come on, it's time to go."

Elizabeth wanted to explain to her sister that she needed more time with her thoughts, but sensing the urgency in the moment she took off, running hand in hand with Margaret. The girls rushed over to a shining black car with some sort of large cat as the emblem. Emmaline was standing by the open back door of the car.

"There you are," she scolded. "First Margaret disappears and now you. Come on, it's time to go," she said to the two girls, who were both dressed alike except Margaret's hat and outfit was boysenberry pink.

Margaret slid into the backseat of the car first, next to their mother and Winston who were already seated. Her mother had on one of her finest white winter dresses. Long sparkling diamond earrings ornamented each ear, and her dark hair was tied back in a tightly styled bun. As Elizabeth slid in next to her sister, she looked up to find that she didn't recognize the figure or the face of the driver.

"That's not Vernon!" Elizabeth squawked out loud. She looked first at Emmaline and then at her mother for an explanation.

"We're late, Elizabeth," Emmaline reminded her as the car pulled from the driveway and onto the main road. As they drove down their street one last time, everyone saw that the house was now surrounded by photographers and news reporters.

"Mother, I don't understand," Elizabeth insisted, "why couldn't Vernon just take us like he always does?"

"Vernon won't be coming, Lilibet," her mother answered. "Only official palace chauffeurs will be driving us from now on."

"But, Mother, that's not fair," Elizabeth protested. "Vernon has always been with us; we can't move without him."

"These are all changes that we have to get used to, Elizabeth. It's the position your uncle has left everyone in," her mother said with frustration.

There was no use in putting up a fight, Elizabeth could tell. She watched as her life and home at 145 Piccadilly got so far behind them that she couldn't see them at all. She knew that she could never go back, and she knew that her life would never be the same.

CHAPTER THREE

The Gloomy Arrival

The short ride to Buckingham Palace seemed to drag on forever. Spirits were low and tensions were running high inside the car.

"Well, girls, welcome to our new abode," her mother said unenthusiastically.

Both Elizabeth and Margaret leaned over Emmaline's shoulder to look at the palace as the car pulled through the imperial gates.

"Is Father here now?" asked Margaret.

Elizabeth looked up to see the Union Jack flag flying at half-mast just above the palace. She knew this meant that there was no monarch in residence.

"No", said Elizabeth drearily, "Father isn't here."

"Alright then, come on, everyone", said their mother. "Let us get out of this car. I want all of us to have selected a bedroom before tea time."

The stranger, now known as their new driver, opened the backdoor of the car and the whole family made their way onto the grounds of their new home. As they all trooped indoors, the words "We want a king!" were heard being chanted from anonymous hostile voices that surrounded the palace.

Once inside, a few of the palace butlers and housemaids greeted them and ushered the family to the living quarters so that they could get right to the business of settling in. Elizabeth and Winston slipped away from the rest of the family and ventured in a different direction. They made their way over to the working side of the palace. Elizabeth floated past one glorious stateroom after another. She had been to Buckingham many times before, but today she saw the palace in a whole new light. The building looked so big and unfamiliar in many ways.

Elizabeth looked into what she knew was called the Centre Room located on the east side of the building. She had so enjoyed all of the times in her earlier childhood when her grandfather would take her onto the balcony of the Centre Room for a quick look at all of London.

Elizabeth continued to travel across to the north side of the palace and entered into her grandfather's old three stories high reading room. She thought about how she and Margaret always called it a library because of how big it was. Bookshelves so tall they could have been made for giants seem to run for miles across the walls of the room. The books were just sitting there collecting dust and it was apparent to Elizabeth that Uncle Eddie hadn't done much reading during his one year at the palace. Everything was just as her grandfather had left it. She remembered the days she'd spend in the library with her grandfather. He'd let her choose as many books as she wanted to read and for hours the two of them would sit on the floor over by the fireplace and read about great adventures and all the mysteries of the universe.

Casting another look around the room, she spotted a silver-framed picture sitting atop the desk where her grandfather often sat at night to do his reading. The photograph featured her grandfather and grandmother, Queen Mary, happily married in their younger years. In a very yearning manner, Winston began scratching at the lowest drawer on the desk. Elizabeth knew what Winston was looking for. It used to be that her grandfather would keep a few liver-flavored duck biscuits in the bottom drawer for any dog visiting the palace.

"Forget about it, Winston", she said bitterly. "He's not here anymore, there's nothing there for you."

Winston whimpered as he followed her out of the reading room. Elizabeth was heading back to where the family was when on the way one more room caught her eye. Elizabeth walked into the giant hall and found herself in what she felt might have been the most exquisite of all the 775 rooms. From the floor to proscenium ceiling, the whole room was a radiant shade of red, decorated with theatrical crimson curtains, and accented by gold detailing. "It's the throne room," Elizabeth captivatedly whispered aloud. As many times as she had been to the palace before she had never actually seen the throne room, but had heard about it in great detail from others over the years. Elizabeth slowly made the long walk up to the canopy that arched over the pair of red thrones. Her eyes had been drawn to them from the moment she entered the room. She thought about what it would be like to see her father and mother sitting there. Then she thought about what life would be like when she would have to sit there. Elizabeth looked around to make sure nobody was nearby. Certain that she was alone, she walked up the red-carpeted steps and sat on one of the thrones. The seat was large enough to make Elizabeth feel like a small speck as her feet dangled over the edge. She thought about how much more comfortable she'd feel if Margaret could be the one to sit on the throne next to hers one day. But she knew this was impossible. She then looked up at a portrait on the wall of her grandparents sitting in the same Chairs of Estate. Elizabeth did her best to imitate her grandfather's regal posture in hopes that it would make her feel more like a queen. She even tried to replicate her grandfather's earnest facial expression. Winston looked impressed as he wagged his tail at the sight of little Elizabeth sitting on the throne. But Elizabeth quickly slumped in her posture and slid down in the giant chair.

"Who am I kidding Winston?" she said, "this will never work." Winston walked up the steps to the throne to lick her hand.

Elizabeth then overheard her mother's voice talking to the movers and the head butler out in the hallway. "Okay, now that you've got all of the master bedroom items unloaded, you can get started on unloading the children's items."

"Come on, Winston," Elizabeth rushed, "we better hurry and get sorted." Elizabeth and Winston headed back to the family's living quarters. When arriving, she came across a bedroom with an open door and decided to inspect it as a possible choice for herself, but when she looked inside, she found Margaret jumping up and down on the bed like a professional acrobat.

"Hey Lil," said Margaret in mid-flight, "I like this room, can I keep it?"

"Sure," said a detached Elizabeth, "I'll just go find another one." Elizabeth made her way further up the lengthy hall and turned into the first unoccupied bedroom she could find. The room was large and magnificent but Elizabeth felt somber and unimpressed by it. She did, however, decide to settle for the space. She searched the room in hopes of finding some existence of a secret passageway. Ideally, one that would conveniently lead to Margaret's room. But as grand as the room looked, it failed to be impressive enough to have any secrets about it. She went over to her window and looked out. A flock of pigeons, that seemed to have emerged from the rooftop flew over her window and off into the distance of the late afternoon sky. It looked to Elizabeth like they were flying in the direction that would lead right back to 145 Piccadilly. Elizabeth wished she could fly back to her home with them.

CHAPTER FOUR

Friendly Encounters

Several days passed by, and Elizabeth had hardly left her new room.

"Elizabeth, you've got this wonderful massive bedroom all to yourself. Are you going to lie there and mope forever?" Emmaline asked Elizabeth, who was sitting on her bed, staring blankly at the ceiling.

Elizabeth shrugged, "There's nothing to do here," she solemnly insisted. "It's nothing like Piccadilly. Passersby are outside the palace, angrily shouting all the time. I'm not allowed to play in most of the rooms here and I haven't been horse-riding in weeks. Not to mention, Vernon is gone and Father's not here either."

"You just have to give it time," Emmaline said. "Things will get back to normal, well sort of. In fact, I predict that in a little more time, you'll have found plenty around here to do."

Elizabeth still didn't look convinced.

"Look, I don't want you worrying about ole Vernon, he can look after himself. And as for your father, I've actually received word that he'll be arriving here in a couple of weeks for the ceremony."

Elizabeth's face lit up for the first time in a while at the news of her father's return.

"That's more like it," Emmaline said. "Now I don't want to see you sitting in this room for one more minute. I'm ordering you to go out and play for the rest of the afternoon. Just be back before the Welcoming Ball starts tonight."

Elizabeth sighed, as she doubted whether there would actually be anything for her to do outside, but she did as she was told. She and Winston made their way out to a small picnic area along the edges of the palace, where she found a nice shady tree to sit beneath. She thought about what she could do for the day, but nothing came to mind. Just as she thought about asking Emmaline if she could go back to her room, Elizabeth felt something like a small rock bounce off the top of her head.

"Ouch," she reached down to pick up the pebble-like object from the ground. "It's an acorn," she said aloud. Winston raised up on his hind legs and began barking up the tree. "Winston, don't be ridiculous," Elizabeth scolded, "it's probably just a squirrel or something."

"No, it's not a squirrel," a voice said, coming from the tree.

"Who said that?" demanded a startled Elizabeth.

"I said it," the voice answered back. A girl about the same height and age as Elizabeth, with strawberry-tinted hair, green eyes, and freckles jumped out of the tree. "Sorry about the acorn," she said. "I accidentally knocked it down when I was up there."

"Who are you?" asked Elizabeth.

"I'm Pam, Pamela Sunsprite," said the smiley, tomboy-ish-looking girl. They shook hands.

"I'm Elizabeth."

Pam's eyes nearly popped out of her head. "So, you're the princess who just moved here that everyone keeps making a fuss about?"

"Sure, I guess," replied Elizabeth.

"Your Uncle Edward has sure caused a ruckus through-out the country," Pam sarcastically continued.

"Don't I know it," said Elizabeth. "What were you doing up in that tree anyways?"

"Playing hide-and-go-seek," answered Pam.

"You should meet my sister Margaret," said Elizabeth. "She's the best at hiding-and-seeking, too. Who's trying to find you?"

"I'm hiding from my pal, Devi. Hey, Devi," called out Pam, "I'm over here."

Another young girl with a flowing pink and purple sari and long, dark hair, came from around a distant pillar in the area. She appeared to be of about the same age as that of Elizabeth and Pam.

"Would it have killed you to wait a little longer for me to find you?" Devi asked as she made her way over to where they were standing.

"Will you believe it? While you were trying to find me, I found a princess," Pam bragged.

Devi turned around with a dumbfounded smile on her face. She looked at Elizabeth as if she were a magnificent mysterious present under a Christmas tree. "My goodness, you're the new princess that everyone said was moving here!" she gasped. "The whole palace was waiting on you to arrive."

"The whole palace?" asked Elizabeth.

"Well sure," continued Devi. "And I've also read everything there is to read about you in the newspapers. You're the talk of the town. I read all about how your uncle gave up being king all because an unlikely sorceress from a faraway land put a dark spell on him that can't be broken, and how your father is a muttering loon, but now the fate of the whole kingdom is on the shoulders of you and your family as we head into an era of grave danger, and then if we survive it all one day you'll become our queen. It's a really amazing story!" Devi exclaimed gleefully." "William Shakespeare couldn't have written it any better himself."

Elizabeth and Pam stood speechless over how awkward Devi's long-winded synopsis of current events made their whole encounter feel.

"I beg your pardon?" asked Elizabeth.

"Uh, you'll have to excuse her," Pam nervously apologized. "Devi here has never met a princess before. Sometimes she's a little away with the fairies. It'd probably be for the best if we left now." Pam pulled Devi along by the arm in hopes of escaping the uncomfortable situation.

"Wait," Elizabeth called. "What else have the papers been saying?"

That question led them into a very long discussion.

The three girls sat in the picnic area and chatted for hours. Eventually, they got around to talking about other things. Pam told stories about how her elder brother Peter had been teaching her to sword fight and how she dreamt of being a great sword handler like many of her other family members back in Braemar. Devi talked about the first time she attempted to ride a horse, only to realize that she had mounted a mule instead. And Elizabeth told them all about how she had first found out that she and her family would be moving to Buckingham Palace. She also shared about how much she missed Vernon, and how she'd probably never see Uncle Eddie again. Most of all she talked about her days at 145 Piccadilly. She told them all about Castle York and even about the secret passageway she had that led from her room to Margaret's. Elizabeth had never told anyone about that before. The girls sat in silence for a moment after learning about all Elizabeth had been through.

"Look at it this way," said Pam. "You sure gave up a lot, but, at least, you'll have a queendom to show for it one day."

"I guess," said Elizabeth. "But there's just so much to learn. I wouldn't know the first thing about running a country. And it's so hard knowing that everyone is watching every little thing I do. What will people think if I make mistakes? I'm worried about my father, and I can tell he's scared. I'm scared too, really. Our life was so uncomplicated before, now it's not."

"And to think, all this time I thought being royal meant having fun all day and doing what you wanted. Guess I was wrong. It's so awful that you didn't even get to say goodbye to your friend Vernon," said Devi as she patted Elizabeth on the shoulder for comfort.

In the midst of the conversation, Elizabeth noticed that someone was missing. "Where's Winston?" she asked.

"Who is Winston?" Devi replied.

"That's Winston!" shrieked Pam, as she frantically pointed across the paved footpath to expose Winston digging up a bed of tulips.

The girls ran over to see the mess he was making. "Oh no!" Pam said in horror. "My father planted those for your uncle not long before he left."

"Gosh, I'm so sorry about this," Elizabeth said as she gave a disapproving look at Winston.

"It's ok," Pam replied, "the incoming winter frost would have battered them anyways."

"Did you say that your father planted these?" Elizabeth inquired.

"Yes," said Pam. "Me, my mother, father, and brother, all work here as groundskeepers."

"Does that mean you live here?"

"I sure do," answered Pam, "just not in the fancy part that you stay in. My family and I live on the south end of the grounds. It's where most of the help stays."

"And what about you?" Elizabeth enthusiastically asked Devi.

"I don't live here," Devi said. "My parents work at the Indian embassy just down the road a bit. I come here often on my days off from school. My family has meetings here at the palace all the time."

Elizabeth didn't say anything but deep down she couldn't help but feel excited knowing that Pam and Devi lived so close by. It wasn't often that Elizabeth got to freely mingle with other kids her own age.

"So," Devi said, unintentionally changing the subject, "what's your favorite thing about living here at Buckingham so far?"

"Devi, haven't you heard anything the gal's been telling us all this time? She's practically homesick," Pam butted in.

"Oh, sorry," Devi said to Elizabeth. "I didn't mean to make you feel worse, I can be a bit clumsy sometimes."

"It's alright," said Elizabeth sadly, "it's not your fault. There's nothing anyone can do about it anyways."

"Well," Devi chimed back in attempting to lighten the mood, "you must at least be excited for the big party tonight."

"Party?" Elizabeth asked.

"Sure, the Welcoming shindig palace officials will be throwing for your family tonight. I've always wanted to go to one. They're said to be amazing," Devi explained.

"Oh, the Welcoming Ball!" gasped Elizabeth, "I almost forgot about it. Will either of you be there?" she asked.

"'Fraid not," answered Pam. "My family and I have got a lot of work to do between now and your father's coronation ceremony."

"I can't either," said Devi, "the last of the Diwali festivities are tonight at the embassy. But you'll probably see our other friend Jade there. She's usually at all the palace events."

"I'll keep an eye out for her then," said Elizabeth. "It's been a pleasure to meet both of you, but I better get going. Emmaline and my mother will have a fit if I'm late for the ball tonight." Elizabeth waved goodbye to her new friends as she and Winston hurried inside the palace. The girls felt so at ease with each other that neither of them realized they had forgotten to curtsy to Elizabeth.

"See you again soon," Devi called after the briskly moving princess.

"She seems like a nice enough lass," Pam said to Devi.

The ball was everything Pam and Devi had speculated it would be and more. Dazzling food dishes that filled the room with mouthwatering aromas, and colorful holiday trifles lined the table from one end to the other. There were lavish Christmas decorations from wall to wall, and everyone in attendance was wearing exquisite outfits. The music of London's best orchestra filled the night air. Elizabeth stood in a corner near the exit while her mother effortlessly regaled the room. Margaret did a bit of schmoozing herself while Emmaline kept a close eye on her. Elizabeth watched as the night went on. She thought about the wonderful, smaller Christmas parties thrown by her family at their old home. Just as she thought about retiring early from the party, a very debonair-looking girl walked over to her. Dressed in a beautiful sparkling red dress, her tightly coiled hair was pulled back and held in a fluffy ponytail by a pearly garnished comb.

"You don't look like you're having much fun," the girl said.

"I hardly know anyone here," Elizabeth responded.

"That hasn't stopped your sister any," the girl answered back. They both looked over at Margaret chatting up a very important-looking man by the dessert table.

"My father looks like his ear is going to fall off," the girl giggled.

"That's your father?" Elizabeth asked.

"Yes, that's him," the girl confirmed. "He serves as one of the royal advisors to the reigning monarch along with Sir Reginald Phifer. And that's my mother talking to your mum. My mother was lady-in-waiting to your grandmother, Queen Mary. She'll now be a lady-in-waiting to your mother, Her Majesty Elizabeth. It's kind of neat how you and your mother both have the same name."

"How did you know that she's my mother?" asked Elizabeth. "And how did you know about our names?"

"I'm psychic," the girl said. Elizabeth looked flabbergasted. "I'm only kidding," the girl chuckled. "Actually, my name is Jade," she said, "and you're the new Princess. Pamela

Sunsprite told me that you'd be here tonight. She asked me to help you get familiar with everything here at the palace."

"Oh, no wonder," said Elizabeth. "You must know Pam and Devi really well."

"I do," replied Jade. "I've known Devi for a couple of years, ever since her family began working for the embassy. And I've known Pam my whole life. We were both born and raised right here in the palace you know."

The two girls went on to bond that night over many plates of creamy delicious trifle. Elizabeth listened in astonishment to how much Jade knew about palace life and about all the fun she and the other girls had there. The two even shared a few laughs by swapping embarrassing stories about Prime Minister Baldwin that they had witnessed firsthand. Elizabeth found Jade to be very poised and sophisticated for a girl of just ten.

"So how are you liking it here?" Jade asked.

Elizabeth dropped her head and focused on the tips of her shoes. "To be honest, I miss my old home," she answered.

She told Jade all about how she missed Vernon and about her life back at 145 Piccadilly, while Jade attentively listened.

"Wow," Jade said. "Piccadilly sounds like an amazing place to live."

"It is," Elizabeth happily responded. "I mean it was," she sadly corrected herself.

"Buckingham can be a great place too, you know," Jade said, "just give it a chance. In time, you'll feel right at home here. And given your future circumstances," Jade added, "the sooner you feel at home here the better."

Elizabeth gave an anguish-filled nod in agreement. She was enjoying Jade's company, and she knew that Jade was right. But feeling at home in Buckingham still felt too far from possible.

CHAPTER FIVE

The <u>Oaths</u> of Coronation Day

The countdown to the Duke of York's coronation was on. At the very least, the entire country had gone haywire, if not the whole world. Newspapers had no shortage of new stories to print on the matter. Bakeries all over the island prepared special pastries for the occasion. Street parties kicked off early in small villages and city boroughs. Miles of colorful, home-made bunting dressed the streets of every neighborhood. It was as if each town was in competition with one another to prove who could be the most festive. Elderly citizens had non-stop celebratory tea parties in their front yards, while the pubs never slept. Inspired by the pints of rum running through their veins, brutish gentlemen and carefree maidens were steadily coming up with new patriotic songs to chant in honor of the new king. There were hardly enough barrels of rum, ale, and brandy to be kept in stock. Hundreds of thousands of spectators, both rich and poor, old and young, staked out the streets that were the intended route of the procession. Even the smallest of boys and girls camped along the roads for days and nights. They all hoped to catch a glimpse of their favorite royals during the grand procession that would take place on the big day. Meanwhile, the Archbishop of Canterbury was busy overseeing all the tedious preparations at Westminster Abbey. The Duke's crowning and taking of the sacred oath would be held at the ancient church, just as so many other royal coronations had been for over a thousand years.

Inside palace walls, Elizabeth and Margaret had no shortage of non-stop dress measurements, tiara fittings, and etiquette trainings. Grandmother Mary saw to it that they attended every single one of them. Even Winston had to receive a royal grooming. Once in a while, Elizabeth would catch a glimpse of Jade, Pam, and Devi about the palace as she was being rushed from one appointment to another. She was always sure to wave in passing but wished for only a brief moment to leave all the formal chaos behind and play with them. They always seemed to be up to something interesting and Elizabeth wanted to join.

The staff worked tirelessly around the clock to make sure everything was in place. King's Guards polished their shoes to take part in the march, while court jesters readied themselves to entertain the masses. All the hustle and bustle made Elizabeth dizzy.

By some miracle, Coronation Day finally arrived. Elizabeth had been awakened in the morning not by Emmaline, but by the sound of the official royal cannons being fired off to announce the beginning of the occasion. The whole morning Elizabeth fidgeted with her dress. The lace caused a horrible itch that wouldn't go away. But once seated inside Westminster Abbey, Elizabeth forgot all about the nuisance that was her coronation dress. She kept a close watch on both of her parents as her father, and then her mother received their crowns. She saw how nervous they looked. Both of them made every movement with extreme caution, especially her father. Elizabeth crossed her fingers and hoped that all would go well, and so it did.

Afterward, Elizabeth and Margaret loaded into the horse-drawn carriage that would take them from Westminster back to the palace. The parade seemed to stretch all the way across London.

Elizabeth and Margaret watched as children gleefully raced on foot alongside their golden coach, cheering the princesses on. Elizabeth took great pleasure in watching the families standing on the streets, all celebrating this hopeful day with one another. It reminded her of all the simple happy times she had once had with her family. She feared it might never be that way again.

Upon arrival, the first thing Elizabeth noticed was the Royal Standard flag flying high above the palace instead of the Union Jack. This signified to all that the reigning monarch was indeed at Buckingham. Seeing the flag brought an overwhelming wave of excitement over both Elizabeth and Margaret. Finally, their father was home, after weeks of being away preparing for his new job.

Elizabeth and Winston bounded into the Centre Room for what would be the end of the world-famous ceremony.

"Lilibet, dogs don't belong in the Centre Room!" her mother scolded.

"Here, I'll get him out of the way," said Emmaline. But before she could reach the pup, Statesman Churchill had made his way over and scooped Winston up from the floor and into his arms.

"Leave him be," he warned, "I love dogs." The spry old man gave Winston a tickle behind the ears. "I must say, this is a delightful Corgi, whatever might his name be?" Elizabeth, her mother, and Emmaline, all held their breath while blushing.

"Uh, it's kind of a family joke, sir," Elizabeth insisted nervously, "you wouldn't get it."

"Oh, ok then," said an unsuspicious Mr. Churchill. He merrily carried Winston over to a cart of finger sandwiches for them to share.

The room was full of important political figureheads and royals from other nations. Many of her aunts, uncles, and cousins were present too, as well as members of the royal staff. Elizabeth even spotted Sir Reginald and Jade's father, Mr. Devonshire, chatting with Grandmother Mary in the corner, who was still scowling about not forgiving Uncle Eddie. Meanwhile, Devi's parents, the Singhs, could be found speaking with Mrs. Devonshire about the possibility of Mr. Churchill running for Prime Minister in the near future. Mr. and Mrs. Sunsprite, along with their son, Peter, were out on the ground level in front of the palace, opening the gates to allow members of the public to get a closer view of the royal balcony. Everyone at Buckingham was dressed in their royal best.

"Where's Father?" Elizabeth asked her mother. "I'm certain he's here."

"Here he is," said a voice that was nearing the inside of the Centre Room. It was Prime Minister Baldwin dressed in a spiffy burgundy suit, and stepping in right behind him was her father, draped in a beautiful, red, royal mantle. He looked statelier than anyone had ever seen him before. Elizabeth and Margaret raced over to congratulate him on finally coming home. This was the first chance they'd gotten to embrace him the entire day, even though the girls had been able to watch his crowning ceremony from afar earlier in the day. He was careful when leaning down to hug them to keep his newly-placed crown from falling. There was so much that Elizabeth had to say to him, but her mother took her by the hand before she could even speak. Elizabeth, her mother, Margaret, Grandmother Mary, and her father, each of their heads crown adorning, stepped out as one onto the royal balcony. There was a great roar from the crowd as Elizabeth and the new royal family overlooked the sea of people. What seemed to be all of Great Britain had shown up! Flags from every nation of the commonwealth were being twirled in the air. Looking at the droves of passionate well-wishers was daunting for the shy Elizabeth; so self-conscious she reached up to make sure her crown was still in place. She glanced over at her sister passionately waving at the adoring crowds as if she was at the sporting match of the century. Something started to feel heartwarming about it all to Elizabeth. Perhaps Margaret had been right all along about everything working out for the best. The crowd chanted with a renewed sense of joy as they continued to cheer on their new king and his family.

"Long Live King George the VI," they cried out, "Long live King George!" Elizabeth's heart instantly broke. When they came in from the balcony, she could no longer wait to speak to her father after what she had just heard. She tugged at his hand and he looked down to see the burning concern in his daughter's eyes. He knelt down low to make sure he could hear her.

"Father," she said, "why does everything have to change?"

"How do you mean?" he asked. Usually, he stumbled over his words, but the warmth of his daughter's presence had a way of smoothing his speech.

"Well, first we lose Grandfather, then we move from Piccadilly, we no longer have Vernon, and now everyone is calling you George. What's wrong with Albert?" she cried. "It's a perfectly nice name, it's your name, and I don't want to think of you as anyone else."

"Oh, c-come on now," he said with a hearty laugh. "George is a much more s-suitable English-sounding name, d-don't you think? Albert makes me sound like I just waltzed out of Bavaria or something, and we can't have that now, c-can we?" Elizabeth didn't reply, and the gentle king could see the worry was all too much for his darling princess almost as shy as he. The matter was too serious for him to simply fix with a lighthearted tease. "You're right, Lilibet, a lot of changes have happened to this family in recent times. It hasn't been easy on me either, but I remind myself every day that change is not always a bad thing."

"But, Father," Elizabeth said, "everyone will be watching me from now on. Even more than before, they'll be watching to see what I do right and what I do wrong."

"And they'll be watching me, too," he interrupted. "You don't think I hear some of the whispers about your dear, old dad around here? I know a lot of people feel that ole Bertie isn't fit for the job."

"Then why are you choosing to stay?" asked Elizabeth.

"B-because it's not about me," he answered. "It's about my responsibility to the people of this land. Do you know why I took the name George?" he asked.

"Perhaps you like your middle name better than your first all of a sudden, or maybe it's something your advisors told you to do?"

The king chuckled at his daughter's facetious humor as it was something she rarely displayed. "I took the name George because it was your grandfather's name. He was a reliable man and right now the people need to be reminded of what it feels like to have a king that will never forsake them. War is coming to England sooner or later and they'll need a king they can count on. One day, my Lilibet, they'll count on you just the same."

As upset as she wanted to allow herself to feel, it was impossible for her not to respect what her father had decided his life should stand for. "I'll never leave them either," she replied. Her father smiled.

It seemed as if the crowd's chanting grew louder and louder outside of the palace. "Your people are calling for you, Your Majesty," Prime Minister Baldwin said, playfully pestering King George.

"Well," Elizabeth's father said kissing her on the cheek, "duty awaits me. But if I were you, I'd take a quick peek in the hallway," he suggested. Her father gave her a wink, then he and her mother, the new queen consort, stepped out onto the balcony for another appearance before the kingdom. Elizabeth watched from behind the curtains to see their silhouettes wave to the crowds. Confused by what could possibly be in the hallway, Elizabeth quickly and quietly made her way over to the doorway and took a peep. There in the corridor stood a figure and a humble face she immediately recognized.

"Vernon!" she cried as she rushed over to him.

Margaret had already spotted him and was chatting up a storm. Elizabeth noticed his eyebrow had returned to its relaxed state as he removed his hat and bowed his head to her.

"What are you doing here?" she asked. "I thought we'd never see you again!"

"Hello, Your Royal Highness," he said lovingly. "It's all a very long story. But usually, there's an official royal chauffeur that gets to service the king and his family. Your father, being the kind soul that he is, came and found me. A few strings were pulled, and now I've officially been made a royal chauffeur."

Elizabeth wanted to hug him more than anything, but she dared not break royal protocol in front of so many people, and he knew it too. Just at that moment, she heard a voice call her name. She turned around to find that it was Jade rushing to her wearing a stunning purple velvet gown.

"Jade, this is our driver, the one I was telling you about! My father has brought him back home to us!" Elizabeth exclaimed.

"Pleased to meet you, Miss Jade," Vernon said.

"Pleased to meet you, Vernon," Jade said politely while attempting to mask the fact that she was in a rush. "I'm sorry to pull her away, but I have to borrow Elizabeth for a moment."

Elizabeth looked back at Vernon.

"Go on, my lady," he said. "I'll always be here when you return."

Jade continued to pull Elizabeth away, and Margaret ran after them.

"Where are we going?" Elizabeth asked, feeling very out of breath.

"You'll see when we get there," Jade responded. By hand, Jade led Elizabeth and a trailing Margaret across to the north side of the palace and into her grandfather's private library. Right away Elizabeth felt disappointed.

"Who cares about dusty old books?" asked Margaret.

"This is what you wanted to show me? Our grandfather's old book collection?" Elizabeth asked, scratching her head.

"Not exactly," said Jade, who then opened a small drawer on the desk and pulled out a tin box of matches. She struck one across the bottom of her shoe and lit an old candle-burning lantern that had been left on the former king's reading desk. "This is what I wanted to show you," she said. With all of her weight and might, she pushed an old dusty bookcase away to the left side. On the wall behind it hung a large acrylic portrait of Queen Victoria. Jade tugged at the golden edges of the portrait. When pulled back a secret door was revealed.

"Now that's stellar!" Margaret whispered to her sister.

Jade looked back at a stunned Elizabeth and said with a bit of
mystery in her voice, "Turns out that you two weren't the only
ones with a secret passageway." Jade held the lantern up to her
face. The glow of the flame put a shine on her chestnut brown
cheeks. "Stay close," she said as she stepped into the dark

open space, "I'll lead the way." Margaret optimistically strode in after her. Elizabeth stood in the dimly lit library, feeling as if she should probably return to the coronation celebration.

"Come on, Lilibet," Margaret called in her usual fear-less tone. Elizabeth wanted to turn back, but she missed the feeling of having adventures with her sister the way they used to. She, as well, stepped into the dark doorway. Jade shut the portrait door behind them, and now the only light left in the echo-filled drafty space was from the rusty old lantern she carried. They took an old spiral staircase quite a ways down that eventually ended at a gray concrete wall. Here there was a creaky, old, plain-looking, average-sized door with tarnished hinges and a black, ringed door handle made of iron.

"Alright, are you ready?" asked Jade.

Elizabeth shook her head yes, although she did not have the faintest idea of what Jade thought she should be ready for. As far as Elizabeth was concerned, nothing more than an old broom closet could possibly have been behind the unintriguing-looking door.

Jade blew out the candle, leaving the girls in pitch black. The sudden darkness startled both Elizabeth and Margaret, and it made them grasp each other's hands. The door made a groaning sound as Jade pulled the old, welted, wooden door back. In an instant, a burst of light washed over everything in the stairwell. The light shone so brightly that it was almost blinding. The three girls covered their faces to block out the harsh illumination. Stepping out onto a brick pathway, they followed the short trail through a pair of arched metal gates and found themselves surrounded by what looked like a beautiful, enchanted garden that was littered with a light snowfall. The brick path trailed throughout the lush space. Different flowers, plants, weeds, and even a few trees grew in every spot of the green escape. Bare stocks of summer flowers such as cosmos, hollyhock, foxglove, wisteria, catmint, and so many others pushed through the snow. Some plants still held on with a little life left in them. English roses of different colors were planted all around the edges of the enclosure.

In the middle of the garden sat an old cracked marble fountain. The pouring water in the fountain had turned to large beads of ice and slush due to the cold English weather. This created the look of tiny crystals and diamonds flowing from the fountain tiers. To the left of the bush of English roses sat a garden shed that looked like a little stone cottage.

Elizabeth's eyes quickly caught sight of a wooden sign on a pole in the rose bush that had the following words carved on it: Welcome to 145 Piccadilly. Glass mosaic stepping stones outlined the perimeter of the garden shed. The rustic, Dutch door to the stone fixture opened and Pam and Devi walked out holding gardening tools, smiling at Elizabeth.

Elizabeth made her way around the garden and even passed a croquet pitch that looked newly placed. Elizabeth was almost certain that there was something magical about the quad for even in winter the garden overflowed with greenery.

"What is this paradise?" Elizabeth asked.

"Your grandfather used to come here all the time before he took ill," Jade said, who was now standing under some surviving wisteria. "No one's come here since."

"It's beyond amazing, but won't palace officials be mad that royal grounds have been tampered with?" asked Elizabeth.

"They would have to know about this place to be mad," said Pam. "It's George the V's forgotten courtyard. Your grandfather had my parents take it off the palace maps a long time ago so that it could remain his secret place."

"If you like it, then it's yours," said Jade.

"It looks just like our garden back at Piccadilly!" Elizabeth exclaimed.

"It's even got the magic castle!" Margaret sang out, who was now looking inside of the decorated shed.

"We thought we got the details right," Pam said.

"I don't understand," continued Elizabeth, "how could you have managed this? And why would you do it all?"

"Well, Pam got the keys for the supplies, and we all pitched in. I guess we just figured that if you had a space of your own to remind you of Piccadilly, then you might be happier here," said Devi.

"Besides," added Jade, "you're one of us now; there's no need to feel alone. Just as your father did, we as well all took an oath earlier today. We swore for the good of the country and the commonwealth that we'd help you become the most astonishing ruler this kingdom has ever seen. That way, when the time comes, you'll be ready."

"What did I tell you?" said Margaret, now standing near the rest of the girls. "Elizabeth the Great they'll call you."

Elizabeth looked at the garden in amazement and then turned to look at the crew who had pulled together just for her.

She gathered her thoughts for a moment, then managed to utter the announcement: "I think I'll call it Piccadilly Hollow!"

It was obvious to everyone that Elizabeth was finally starting to feel like Buckingham could be her true home. Completely astounded, there was only one thing left that she could say. "Thank you all so much. You have got to be the most amazing friends anyone could have asked for."

"We're like your ladies-in-waiting," Jade said. They all giggled.

"Well, she's not queen yet, so she doesn't exactly need ladies-in-waiting right now. But we could help advise her on things, like a council," said Devi.

"A Piccadilly Council," Margaret, insisted.

Pam reached into her leather scabbard and pulled out a wooden handmade training sword that she used for fencing practice and handed it to Elizabeth. "We should make this official," Pam said. "You'll have to swear us in, like a knighthood."

"I've never knighted anyone," Elizabeth resisted. "Although, I was there to see my grandfather knight, Sir Reginald Phifer, for his years of dutiful service to the crown."

"Perfect, just do what you saw your grandfather do," Pam instructed.

Elizabeth gently rolled the sword around in her hands while contemplating her next move.

"Alright then," said Elizabeth, "everyone should kneel." Pam, Devi, Jade, and Margaret, all bowed their heads and took a knee on a large slab of stone that lay on the ground next to the garden cottage. They formed a circle around

Elizabeth, who straightened the now crookedly- fitting crown on her head and held herself perfectly upright in posture. She gently tapped each girl on the shoulder with the cherry oak sword. "With this being my first task as your future queen, it is my great honor to now pronounce you all keepers of the oath, guardians of the Hollow, and knights of the Piccadilly Council. Now arise," she declared.

Pam, Devi, Jade, and Margaret rose to their feet. Young as they were, the five council members knew that many adventures lay ahead of them. The little queen-to-be couldn't stop beaming from ear to ear as she felt completely lost in the wonder of it all.

"This is going to be too much fun," said Elizabeth.